Sing a Song of Sixpence

Pictures by TRACEY CAMPBELL PEARSON

Dial Books for Young Readers

E. P. Dutton, Inc.   New York

Published by Dial Books for Young Readers
A Division of E. P. Dutton, Inc. / 2 Park Avenue / New York, New York 10016
Published simultaneously in Canada by Fitzhenry & Whiteside Limited, Toronto

Pictures copyright © 1985 by Tracey Campbell Pearson
All rights reserved
Typography by Jane Byers Bierhorst
Printed in Hong Kong by South China Printing Co.
First Edition
W
10 9 8 7 6 5 4 3 2 1

Library of Congress Cataloging in Publication Data

Pearson, Tracey Campbell / Sing a song of sixpence.

Summary/An illustrated version of the traditional
rhyme about the four-and-twenty blackbirds baked in a pie.
1. Nursery rhymes. 2. Children's poetry. [1. Nursery rhymes.] I. Title.
PZ8.3.P2748Si 1985   398'.8   84-14206
ISBN 0-8037-0151-9   ISBN 0-8037-0152-7 (lib. bdg.)

The art for each picture consists of an ink, watercolor, and
gouache painting that is camera-separated and reproduced in full color.

For M. and J.

Sing a song of sixpence,

A pocketful of rye;

Four-and-twenty blackbirds

Baked in a pie;

When the pie was opened,

The birds began to sing;

Wasn't that a dainty dish

To set before the King?

The King was in his countinghouse,
Counting out his money;

The Queen was in the parlor,
Eating bread and honey;

The maid was in the garden,

Hanging out the clothes;

Along came a blackbird,
And snapped off her nose.

But then came a jenny wren,

And popped it on again.

Sing a Song of Sixpence

Sing a song of six-pence, a pock-et ful of rye; Four-and-twen-ty black-birds baked in a pie;

When the pie was o-pened, the birds be-gan to sing; Was-n't that a dain-ty dish to set be-fore the King?

The King was in his countinghouse, counting out his money;
The Queen was in the parlor, eating bread and honey;
The maid was in the garden, hanging out the clothes;
Along came a blackbird and snapped off her nose.